大喜說故事系列

Tashi

and the
DANCING SHOES
大喜與寶鞋

Anna Fienberg 著
Barbara Fienberg

Kim Gamble 繪

王盟雄 譯

三民書局

'One Saturday, Jack invited Tashi for lunch to meet his Uncle Joe.

'He's my father's brother,' Jack told him proudly. 'He's been **traveling** all over the world.'

'That's interesting,' said Tashi. 'I wonder if he's ever been to *my* village.'

'We'll ask him,' Jack said excitedly. 'You can **swap** stories about snake-infested forests and wild **escapes** from war lords. It'll be great!'

某個星期六，傑克邀了大喜一塊兒吃午餐，順便讓他見見喬大叔。

　　「他是我老爸的弟弟，」傑克很神氣地告訴他。「他到世界各地旅行過。」

　　大喜說，「那可好玩了，不知道他有沒有去過我們的村子。」

　　「等一下我們可以問他。」傑克很興奮地說。「你們可以聊聊有毒蛇盤據的森林，也可以談談在督軍追殺下的大逃亡，一定會很有趣！」

travel [`trævl̩] 動 旅行

swap [swɑp] 動 交換

escape [ɪ`skep] 名 逃亡

Tashi and Joe did have a lot to talk about. They talked all through the soup, well into the beef with noodles, **pausing** only when the apple cake was **served**.

'It's very good to meet an uncle of yours, Jack,' said Tashi, taking a bite of his cake. 'Have you got any more?'

'There's some in the kitchen,' said Mom, **hopping** up.

大喜和喬大叔果然聊了很多。從喝湯到吃牛肉麵，話題都不曾間斷，只有在蘋果蛋糕上桌時才暫停下來。

　　「傑克，能夠認識你這位叔叔真是太棒了，」大喜咬了一口蛋糕，問說，「還有嗎？」

　　老媽立刻起身說，「廚房裡還有一些。」

pause [pɔz] 動 暫停
serve [sɝv] 動 上（菜）
hop [hɑp] 動 跳

'He meant *uncles*, Mom,' laughed Jack. 'You know, if we asked all *yours* to lunch, Tashi, we'd have to **hire** the town hall!'

Tashi nodded. 'It's true. But I'll tell you something. No matter if you have forty uncles and fifty-six aunts and nine hundred and two cousins, all of them are **precious**.' He sighed. 'Take Lotus Blossom, for example.'

'Who's that?' asked Dad, **scratching** his head. 'An uncle?'

「老媽，他是說還有別的叔叔嗎？」傑克笑著說。「你知道嗎，大喜，如果要請你所有的叔叔來吃飯的話，我們恐怕得租下整個鎮公所才夠位子呢！」

大喜點點頭。「的確。不過說真的，不管你是有四十位叔叔、五十六位嬸嬸，還是九百零二位表兄弟姊妹，他們通通都很重要。」他嘆了一口氣。「像阿蓮就是。」

「他是誰呀？你叔叔嗎？」老爸搔著頭問。

hire [haɪr] 動 租用
precious [`prɛʃəs] 形 珍貴的
scratch [skrætʃ] 動 搔，抓

9

Tashi scooped up the last of his cake. 'No, Lotus Blossom is my cousin. We used to play **chasings** near the river in summer. *Wah*, was she a fast runner! Nearly quicker than *me*! She'd go streaking off on her own then **hide** in the tiniest, most impossible places. I'd take ages to find her.' Tashi finished up his cake and pushed back his chair. 'So when they told me Lotus Blossom had **disappeared**, I wasn't too worried. At first, that is.'

Uncle Joe leaned forward. 'Disappeared, eh?' He nodded knowingly. 'What was it? Bandits, war lords, *kid**nappers***?'
Dad winked at Jack. 'Here we go!' he whispered, bouncing on his chair.

大喜用湯匙挖起最後一口蛋糕。「不是，阿蓮是我表妹。我們以前夏天的時候常常在河邊追逐嬉戲。哇塞，她可真會跑！簡直比我還快！她會一溜煙兒地跑走，然後躲在最小、最難找到的地方。我總要花個老半天才能找到她。」

大喜吃完蛋糕，把椅子往後一挪。「所以當有人跟我說阿蓮失蹤的時候，我並不是很擔心。至少剛開始時是這樣的。」

喬大叔的身體往前一傾。「哦，失蹤了？」他會意地點點頭。「是誰幹的？歹徒、督軍，還是綁匪？」

老爸對傑克使了個眼色，身體從椅子上坐直，壓著嗓子說，「有故事可聽了！」

chasing [`tʃesɪŋ] 名 追逐
hide [haɪd] 動 躲藏
disappear [ˌdɪsə`pɪr] 動 消失
kidnapper [`kɪdnæpɚ] 名 綁匪

'Well, it was like this,' began Tashi. 'One afternoon, my mother and I had just come back from a visit to Wise-as-an-Owl, when there was a furious **knocking** at the door and Lotus Blossom's grandmother, Wang Mah, **stumbled** in. Her face was wet with tears and strands of hair from her bun were plastered across her cheeks.

"'I've lost her!" Wang Mah **burst out**. "One minute my dear little Lotus Blossom was playing in the courtyard right next to me—the *next*, she was gone!" She **wrung** her hands. "Oh, what will happen when night falls?"

「嗯，事情是這樣子的，」大喜說。「有一天下午，我媽媽和我剛拜訪聰明道人回來，就聽到有人很急地敲門敲個不停。阿蓮的奶奶王媽跌跌撞撞地闖了進來，整張臉沾滿著淚水，好幾絡從髮髻上掉下來的頭髮黏在她的臉頰上。

　　「『她不見了！』王媽哭喊出聲說。『一分鐘前我的小蓮還跟我待在院子裡玩──才一轉眼，她就不見了！』她緊握著雙手。『哦，天黑後不知道會不會發生什麼事？』

knocking [`nɑkɪŋ] 图 敲門聲
stumble [`stʌmbl̩] 動 跌跌撞撞地走
burst out　大叫說
wring [rɪŋ] 動 絞，扭（過去式 wrung[rʌŋ]）

'My mother sat her down on a chair.

'"I was just painting my **screen**," Wang Mah went on. "You know, the one with the Red Whiskered Dragon? Well, I couldn't get the green right on the scales—"

'"Where did you look for her?" I **interrupted**.

'Wang Mah threw up her hands. "Oh, everywhere! The fields, the cemetery—I've told the whole village, practically. Everyone's out looking, but no one can find her. Oh, my little one, where could she be?"

'Well, I knew we wouldn't find her sitting there in the house worrying, so I told my mother that I was going to join the **search party** and that I would be back later.

「我媽媽扶她到椅子上坐下。

「王媽接著說,『我正在給屏風上漆,你知道的,就是那個畫著紅鬚龍的屏風,呃,可是那種綠色怎麼調就是調不出來──」

「『你上哪兒找過她?』我插嘴問。

「王媽揮舞著雙手。『噢,我每個地方都找遍了!農田、墓地──我還幾乎通知了全村的人。大家都出去找了,卻怎麼也找不到。啊,我的小蓮到底到哪裡去了?』

「嗯,我知道光坐在家裡擔心是絕對找不到她的,所以我就跟媽媽說我也要加入搜救隊伍,而且會晚一點回家。

screen [skrin] 名 屏風
interrupt [ˌɪntəˋrʌpt] 動 打斷(談話)
search party 搜救隊伍

'"Oh, thank you, Tashi," cried Wang Mah. "If anyone can find her, you will, I know."

'I wasn't so sure, but I crossed my fingers and gave her the sign of the dragon for luck. But as I walked towards the village square, a cold fear was settling in my stomach. Whenever Grandmother was painting one of her screens, she didn't hear or see anything else for hours. Lotus Blossom might have been missing since **dawn**. So I decided to go at once to the village **fortune teller**.'

「『哦，大喜，謝謝你。』王媽哭著說。『我知道，假如有人能夠找到她的話，那個人一定是你。』

　　「我不敢打包票，但是我祈禱了一下，並對她做了個龍的幸運手勢。可是當我走向村子的廣場時，我的胃卻害怕地打起寒顫。每次老奶奶一畫起屏風，就會好幾個小時聽不到、看不見其他的東西。阿蓮很可能一大早就失蹤了。所以我決定先去找村裡的算命仙。」

dawn [dɔn] 名 黎明

fortune teller 算命仙

Uncle Joe nodded wisely. 'I went to one last year, when I was back in the **tropics**. Did I ever tell you about the time—'

'Yes,' said Dad quickly.

'So, Tashi,' said Mom, 'did the fortune teller have any news?'

'Well, it was like this. Luk Ahed had done **horoscope** charts for everyone in our village, so I thought he might give us a **clue** about Lotus Blossom. Luk Ahed is very good at telling the future, but not so brilliant at keeping things tidy. He **rummaged** through great piles of sacred books and maps of the stars and bamboo sticks. But he couldn't find her horoscope anywhere.

喬大叔明智地點點頭。「去年我回到熱帶地區時就找過一個算命仙。我有沒有跟你提過——」

　　「提過了，」老爸很快地應了一聲。

　　「那麼，大喜，」老媽說，「算命仙那裡有沒有著落？」

　　「這個嘛，事情是這樣的。盧半仙把我們村裡每個人的命盤都排好了，所以我想他或許能提供阿蓮的線索給我們。盧半仙對算命的確有兩把刷子，但是卻不太擅長整理東西。他翻遍了成堆的寶典、星象圖和竹筷，偏偏就是找不到阿蓮的命盤。

tropic [ˋtrɑpɪk] 名 熱帶地區

horoscope [ˋhɔrəˌskop] 名 天宮圖

clue [klu] 名 線索

rummage [ˋrʌmɪdʒ] 動 翻尋

"'I'll start on a new one right away," he
promised. Then he **grunted** with surprise. He
had *my* chart in his hand.

"'Just look at this," he marveled. "I see a great
adventure awaiting you, Tashi, just as soon as
you find a very special pair of red shoes with
green glass peacocks embroidered on them."

「『我馬上重排一張，』」他允諾。緊接著卻驚訝地嘀咕了起來。他手上拿著的正巧是我的命盤。

　　「『過來瞧瞧，』」他驚嘆。『有一場大冒險正等著你唷，大喜，就等你找到一雙很特別的紅鞋子，上面繡著綠色的玻璃孔雀。』」

grunt [grʌnt] 動 咕嚕地說
adventure [əd`vɛntʃɚ] 名 冒險

'I walked out of there very thoughtfully, I can tell you. I could almost remember seeing such a pair of shoes, but where? As I turned the corner into the village I heard the **familiar** rat-a-tat-tat coming from the **shoemaker's** shop.

'"Hello, Tashi," Not Yet called from his open door. Our cobbler was called Not Yet because no matter how long people left their shoes with him, when they **returned** to see if they were ready, he always said, "Not yet. Come back later."

「坦白說，走出那裡時，我的思緒混亂不已。我還依稀記得曾經看過這麼一雙鞋子，可是到底是在哪裡呢？當我拐過牆角走回村子時，我聽到鞋匠鋪裡傳來熟悉的搭搭搭的敲打聲。

　　「『嗨，大喜，』慢爺從敞開的大門向大喜喊道。大家管這鞋匠叫慢爺，因為不管鞋子留在他那裡多久，只要回去看看鞋子修好了沒有，他總是回答，『還沒，待會兒再來。』」

familiar [fə`mɪljɚ] 形 熟悉的
shoemaker [`ʃu͵mekɚ] 名 鞋匠
return [rɪ`tɝn] 動 返回

'Well, I stopped right there on the **doorstep**. Of course, *that's* where I'd seen those strange shoes. I ran into the shop and asked Not Yet if he still had them.

'"I think so," said Not Yet. "I know the ones you mean. They were here when I took over this shop from my father years ago." He **poked around** at the back of the shelves and finally **fished out** a dusty pair of shoes. He **wiped** them clean with his sleeve.

'The shoes were just as I remembered. They were red **satin** and glowed in the dingy room. I took some coins from my pocket and asked, "Could I take them now?"

「我就停在那門階上。對了，我就是在那裡看到那雙怪鞋的。我衝進店裡問慢爺它們還在不在。

　　「『應該在吧，』慢爺說。『我知道你說的那一雙。幾年前我從我老爸手上接管這間店舖時，它們就在這裡了。』他在架子後面翻了翻，最後終於挖出了一雙髒兮兮的鞋子。他用袖子把它們擦乾淨。

　　「鞋子和我記憶中的一模一樣。那紅色的緞子在髒亂不堪的房間裡顯得格外鮮豔。我從口袋裡拿出幾枚硬幣，問說，『我可以現在買下來嗎？』

doorstep [ˋdɔrˏstɛp] 名 門階

poke around 翻找

fish out 取出

wipe [waɪp] 動 擦拭

satin [ˋsætɪn] 名 緞

'Not Yet looked at the **worn** soles and heels and clicked his tongue. "Not yet," he said. "Come back later."

'So I went down to the river for a while and looked along the banks and in our usual hiding places for any **sign** of Lotus Blossom. After an hour, without a speck of dragon luck, I returned to the shop.

'"Be **careful** with them, Tashi," Not Yet said as he handed the shoes to me. "Be *very* careful." And he looked at me in a **worried** way.

「慢爺看看早已磨損的鞋底和鞋跟，嘖嘖兩聲說，
『還不行，待會兒再來。』」

　　「於是我就去了河邊一會兒，沿著河岸以及我們經
常藏匿的地點，找尋阿蓮的下落。一個鐘頭以後，找不
到任何蛛絲馬跡，我只好回到鞋匠舖。

　　「『大喜，小心使用，』慢爺把鞋子交給我時這麼說
著。『要非常、非常小心。』他很擔憂地看著我。

worn [wɔrn] 形 破舊的

sign [saɪn] 名 蹤跡

careful [`kɛrfəl] 形 小心的

worried [`wɝɪd] 形 擔心的

27

'Clutching them tightly to my chest, I ran as fast as I could to the edge of the village. The shoes glowed like small twin **sunsets** in my hand. When I stopped and put them on, my feet began to grow hot and **tingle**. I gave a little **hop**. At least I meant to give a little hop, but instead it was a great whopping *leap*, followed by another and another, even higher. I couldn't help laughing, it felt so strange. I ran a few steps, but each step was a huge **bound**. In a few seconds I had **crossed** the fields and was down by the river again.

「我把它們緊緊抱在胸前，用最快的速度跑到村界。鞋子宛如一對小夕陽般在我的手上閃耀著。等到我停下來穿上鞋子後，我的腳開始發燙刺痛。我試著跳了一下。本來只想跳一下下而已，不料卻彈得好高，接著一跳又一跳，越彈越高。我忍不住笑了起來，感覺好奇怪。我雖然才跑了幾步，但是每一步距離都好遠。才幾秒鐘的時間，我就越過田野，回到了河邊。

sunset [ˋsʌnˏsɛt] 名 日落
tingle [ˋtɪŋgl̩] 動 感到刺痛
hop [hɑp] 名 跳
bound [baund] 名 範圍
cross [krɔs] 動 橫越過

'Well, even though I was so worried about Lotus Blossom, I have to tell you I couldn't help being **excited** about the shoes.'

'Who could?' cried Dad. 'No one would blame you for that!'

'So I decided to run home—just for a minute, you know—and show my family. But those shoes had other ideas! They went on running in quite the **opposite direction**: over the bridge and into the forest. I tried to stop, but the shoes wouldn't let me. I tried to **kick** them **off**, but they were stuck fast to my feet. I was getting very tired, and a little bit **scared**.'

'Who wouldn't be?' said Dad.

'Even I, with my vast experience, would be alarmed by the situation,' put in Uncle Joe.

「嗯，雖然我很擔心阿蓮，但是說真的，這雙鞋子讓我情不自禁地激動了起來。」

「誰都難免如此，」老爸大聲說。「沒什麼好自責的！」

「於是我決定跑回家——一下下就好，你知道的——好讓我的家人開開眼界。可是那鞋子卻有其他的想法！它們朝著反方向一直跑：經過小橋、進入了森林。我試著停下來，可是鞋子就是不聽使喚。我想要把它們踢掉，卻偏偏黏得更緊。弄得我精疲力盡，還有一點兒害怕。」

「誰不怕呢？」老爸說。

喬大叔插嘴說，「即使像我這種看過不少世面的人，碰到這種情況也會大吃一驚的。」

excited [ɪk`saɪtɪd] 形 興奮的
opposite [`ɑpəzɪt] 形 相反的
direction [də`rɛkʃən] 名 方向
kick off 踢掉
scared [skɛrd] 形 害怕的

'Yes, and then I saw the long shadows of the trees and the deepening dusk. Soon it would be dark, and I didn't know where on earth the shoes were taking me.

'Just then I heard a **shout**. The shoes bounded on and stopped suddenly near the edge of a deep pit. A tiger **pit**! I **shivered** deep inside. I'd had quite enough of tigers, remember, when I was **trapped** with one in that wicked Baron's storeroom.'

'Old Baron *bogey*,' muttered Dad.

'A voice **yelped** again, "Is anyone there?" And do you know, it was Lotus Blossom!

「說的也是，然後我看到樹影幢幢、暮靄四起。天就快黑了，而我還不曉得這雙鞋子到底要把我帶到哪裡去。

「就在那個時候，我聽到一聲喊叫。鞋子繼續往前跳，接著突然在一個很深的坑洞旁邊停了下來。老虎洞！我從心底打了個冷顫。我已經受夠老虎了，還記得我曾經在壞地主的儲藏室裡和一隻老虎關在一塊兒吧！」

「大地主那個老渾球，」老爸喃喃說道。

「又有聲音喊著，『有人在嗎？』你們知道嗎？在洞裡面的竟然是阿蓮！

shout [ʃaʊt] 名 叫喊
pit [pɪt] 名 坑洞
shiver [`ʃɪvɚ] 動 發抖
trap [træp] 動 使困於…
yelp [jɛlp] 動 叫

"'Yes, it's me, Tashi!" I called, and the shoes moved forward. I **leaned** over the side of the pit. "Hello, Lotus Blossom. How did you come to **fall** down there? You weren't *hid*ing, were you?"

"'No!" yelled Lotus Blossom, **stamping** her foot. "It's no joke being down here. I got lost, and I was running, and there were **branches** over the pit so you couldn't see it. Oh, Tashi, I've been here all day, so **frightened** that a tiger might come and fall in on top of me."

「『有，是我，大喜！』」我大聲回應後，鞋子又往前跑。我趴在洞的邊緣。『嗨，阿蓮。你是怎麼掉進去的？你該不會是自己躲起來的吧，是嗎？』

　　「『才不是呢！』」阿蓮一邊喊一邊跺著腳。『待在這裡可不是鬧著玩的。我迷路了，慌慌張張地跑著，而這洞上又有樹枝遮住，結果就沒能看個仔細。哎呀，大喜，我已經在這裡待了一整天了。一想到可能會走來一隻老虎，掉下來落在我頭上，就叫我害怕。』

lean [lin] 動 倚靠
fall [fɔl] 動 掉落
stamp [stæmp] 動 跺（腳）
branch [bræntʃ] 名 樹枝
frightened [ˈfraɪtn̩d] 形 害怕的

'I jerked back and shot a look over my shoulder. But what could I do? I had no **rope** or any means of getting her up. Then my toes tingled inside the shoes, reminding me. Yes! My splendid **magic** shoes could take me home in no time and I would be back with a good long rope as quick as two winks of an eye.

'But at that moment Lotus Blossom began to **scream**. My heart thumped as I saw a large black snake slithering down into the hole, **gliding** towards her.

'I didn't have time to think. The shoes picked me up and jumped me down into the pit. *Wah!*

「我猛然往後退，轉過頭去環顧一下四周。可是我又能做什麼呢？手邊既沒有繩子也沒有任何東西能夠把她給弄上來。就在那時候，腳趾在鞋子裡隱隱作痛，我突然靈光一現。對了！神奇的寶鞋馬上就可以帶我回家，只要一眨眼的工夫，我就可以帶來一條又長又堅固的繩子。

　　「不料此時，阿蓮尖叫了起來。我瞧見一條大黑蛇正溜下洞，朝她滑了過去，我的心怦怦怦地直跳。

　　「沒有時間慢慢想了。鞋子將我舉起來，往洞裡栽了下去。哇！

rope [rop] 名 繩子
magic [`mædʒɪk] 形 魔法的
scream [skrim] 動 尖叫
glide [glaɪd] 動 滑行

'Maybe I'll land on the snake and **squash** him, I thought. But no, the snake heard me coming and slid to one side. I landed with a crash.

'"Hide behind me, Lotus Blossom," I said, facing the **serpent**. Lotus Blossom did as I told her, but doesn't she always have to have the last word? She picked up **rocks** and threw them at the snake, shouting *"WAH! PCHAAA!"*

'"Leave him, Lotus Blossom!" I whispered, but it was too late. The snake was enraged. It drove us back into the corner, **lunging** fiercely.

'"Put your arms around my waist and hold on," I told Lotus Blossom.

「我想，也許我會掉在大蛇上面，正好把它壓扁。可惜沒這麼好運。那條大蛇聽到我掉下來，立刻閃到一旁。結果我摔了個狗吃屎。

「面對著大黑蛇，我說，『阿蓮，躲到我背後。』雖然阿蓮照著我的話做了，可是她不是一向都很有主見嗎？她撿起石塊，朝大蛇扔了過去，大喊著，『哇！去你的！』

「『阿蓮，不要理它！』我低聲說，但太遲了。那條蛇火冒三丈，把我們逼進角落，狠狠地撲了過來。

「我告訴阿蓮，『抱著我的腰，抓緊了。』

squash [skwɑʃ] 勔 壓扁
serpent [ˈsɝpənt] 名 蛇
rock [rɑk] 名 石塊
lunge [lʌndʒ] 勔 向前衝

'No sooner had she done so than my feet began to tingle. The magic shoes jumped me straight up the steep side of the pit and out into the clean, fresh air.

'I **hoisted** Lotus Blossom onto my shoulders and with a few exciting bounds we were back in the village square. The bell was rung to call back the searchers, and you should have seen them racing joyfully towards us! They **swept** Lotus Blossom up into their arms, clapping and cheering like thunder. Wang Mah grabbed her, and scolded and wept, her long white hair **tangling** them both together. But when the crowd saw me doing one of my playful little leaps—well, *flying* right over their heads!—they **gasped** in amazement.

「她一照做，我的腳又開始刺痛了起來。那雙寶鞋把我直直舉起，沿著洞穴的陡峭面一躍，就又回到充滿乾淨、新鮮空氣的地面上了。

「我把阿蓮托到肩膀上，奮力跳了幾下，就回到了村子的廣場。鐘聲揚起，把所有搜救的人員都召喚回來。你們應該看看他們興高采烈地向我們跑過來的樣子！他們一把將阿蓮擁進懷裡，同時響起一陣雷鳴般的掌聲和歡呼聲。王媽也抱住阿蓮，一把鼻涕一把眼淚地數落著她的不是，白色的長髮將祖孫兩人纏在一起。但是當大伙兒看到我輕輕一跳——就飛越過大家的頭頂！——他們都驚訝地屏住氣息。

hoist [hɔɪst] 勔 舉起
sweep [swip] 勔 掃入（過去式 swept [swɛpt]）
tangle [ˋtæŋgl̩] 勔 使纏住
gasp [gæsp] 勔 屏息

'"Look at those shoes! Where did he get them? Look at him fly!" they cried.

'I was just taking my bow when I **spied** a face in the crowd that I had hoped never to see again: my greedy Uncle Tiki Pu.'

'Oh, *him!*' Jack turned to Uncle Joe. 'He's the worst uncle ever. When he came to stay with Tashi, he threw all the **toys** out the window to make way for his things!'

'I just brought my pajamas and a change of underpants for the weekend,' said Uncle Joe quickly. 'Is that all right?'

「他們喊著，『看那雙鞋子！他是從哪裡得到的？他在飛呢！』」

「正當我上前接受喝采時，突然瞥見人群中有一張我連看也不想看到的臉：我那貪得無厭的鐵齒布叔叔。」

「哦，是他啊！」傑克把臉轉向喬大叔。「他是世界上最差勁的叔叔。每次他來跟大喜住的時候，都會把所有的玩具扔出窗外，好騰出位置放他自己的東西！」

「我只帶了睡衣，還有過末要換洗的內褲。」喬大叔很快地冒出一句，「這樣可以吧？」

spy [spaɪ] 動 瞥見

toy [tɔɪ] 名 玩具

'When the crowd drifted away,' Tashi went on, 'I walked home. I was feeling very **gloomy**, muttering to myself, when suddenly Tiki Pu's shadow loomed over me. He was **rubbing** his hands together with glee, and my heart sank. But I needn't have worried about him coming to *stay*—that was going to be the least of my problems.

'"You must come to the city with me, Tashi," he said, gripping my shoulder hard. "I know the **Emperor** well. Er, not the Emperor himself, perhaps, but certainly his Master of Revels. He could arrange for you to **dance** at the Palace. We will make our fortunes!"

「大夥兒散去以後，」大喜接著說，「我心情鬱悶地走回家，不斷地喃喃自語。忽然，鐵齒布的身影向我靠了過來。他很得意地摩擦著雙手，而我的心則一直往下沈。其實我那時候根本不需要擔心他會不會住下來——因為有更糟糕的事等在後頭呢！

「『大喜，你一定要跟我進城去。』他緊緊抓著我的肩膀這麼說。『我跟皇帝很熟。呃，也許不是跟皇帝本人，不過肯定是他的寵臣。他可以安排你到皇宮裡跳舞。這樣一來，我們就會發大財了！』

gloomy [`glumɪ] 形 鬱悶的
rub [rʌb] 動 摩擦
Emperor [`ɛmpərɚ] 名 皇帝
dance [dæns] 動 跳舞

'*We* will! *Our* fortunes? I thought.

'Tiki Pu was very **insistent**, never letting me have any peace with all his **jawing** on— "imagine, the *Em*peror, the *Em*peror!"—so in the end I **agreed** to go.

'The next morning, Tiki Pu stood on my toes (yes, it hurt, but at least it was quick) and off we bounded. It was amazing—a **journey** that took days of normal walking was over in half an hour. Suddenly, there we were at the front door of the Emperor's Master of Revels.

「我心裡想著，『發財！我們？』」

「鐵齒布非常堅持，還用他那三寸不爛之舌吵得我不得安寧——『想想看，是皇帝，皇帝呀！』——所以最後我只好答應一起去了。

「隔天早上，鐵齒布就站在我的腳趾上 (這樣的確很痛，但至少這樣子比較快)，我們就一起彈跳起來出發了。真是太神奇了——本來要走好幾天的路程，才半個小時就到了。轉眼間，我們已經在皇帝寵臣的大門口了。

insistent [ɪn`sɪstənt] 形 堅持的
jaw [dʒɔ] 動 嘮叨
agree [ə`gri] 動 同意
journey [`dʒɝnɪ] 名 旅程

'The Master didn't look too **pleased** to see Uncle
Tiki Pu. But after he had watched me do six
somersaults from one leap, and dance up one
wall, across the ceiling and down the other side,
he clapped Tiki Pu on the shoulder.

'"The Emperor is giving a grand dinner tonight,"
he said. "The boy will dance for him at the
Palace."

'Will the Princess Sarashina be there?" I asked.

「那位大臣不怎麼高興看到鐵齒布叔叔，不過在看了我表演跳起來在空中連翻六個觔斗和飛簷走壁以後，他拍了拍鐵齒布的肩膀。

　　「『皇帝今晚要舉辦一場盛大的晚宴，』他說。『這孩子可以去宮殿表演給他看。』

　　「『莎拉喜娜公主也會出席嗎？』我問他。

pleased [plizd] 形 高興的
somersault [`sʌmɚˌsɔlt] 名 觔斗

'"No, she is away visiting her aunt," the Master of Revels called over his shoulder as he hurried away to make the arrangements. Then he stopped. I saw him look back at me, and a **sly** expression came over his face. His eyes **narrowed** into a mean smile.

'We had only gone a little way when the Master came after us. He had two huge evil-looking **guards** with him.

'"Take those shoes from the boy," the Master ordered. "They should fit my son perfectly. He will be much more **graceful**. Why should *this* **clumsy** oaf have the honor of dancing before the Emperor!"

「『不會，她去看她姑媽了，』他丟下這句話，便趕著離開去安排工作。但他卻又突然停下腳步，回頭看著我，臉上浮現狡猾的表情。他的眼睛半瞇，露出卑鄙的眼神。

　　「我們才走了幾步，大臣就追了上來，身邊還多了兩名身材高大、長得一臉兇惡的衛兵。

　　「『把這孩子的鞋子脫下來，』大臣命令著。『如果讓我兒子來穿這雙鞋的話，應該剛剛好，而且看起來會更優雅。這笨手笨腳的傻瓜哪有資格在皇上面前跳舞！』

sly [slaɪ] 形 狡猾的
narrow [`næro] 動 瞇（眼）
guard [gɑrd] 名 衛兵
graceful [`gresfəl] 形 優雅的
clumsy [`klʌmzɪ] 形 笨手笨腳的

'"The Master's honorable son will bring him glory and gold!" said the first guard.

'"Praise and presents!" said the second guard.

'"The shoes won't come off," I said loudly. "I've *tried*."

'The guards rushed at me and pushed and pulled, but they couldn't **remove** the shoes.

'"Oh, well—**chop** off his feet!" ordered the Master. "We can **dig** his toes out of the shoes later."

'I looked **desperately** at my uncle. Tiki Pu took a very small step forward. "Ah," he **stammered**. "You shouldn't really, I mean to say, that's not very—"

'"Be quiet," snapped the Master, "or we will chop off his head, and yours as well."

'Tiki Pu stepped back quickly. "Oh, in that case..."

「『大臣優秀的兒子會為他帶來榮耀和黃金！』第一名衛兵說。

「『還有讚賞和禮物！』第二名衛兵接著說。

「『這雙鞋子脫不下來，』我大聲地說，『我試過了。』

「衛兵撲向我，又拉又扯地，可是鞋子還是脫不下來。

「大臣下令，『噢，好吧——砍斷他的腳！待會兒再把他的腳趾挖出來。』

「我絕望地看著叔叔。鐵齒布往前走了一小步。『呃，你實在不應該，我是說，那樣不是很——』他結結巴巴地說。

「『住口，』大臣厲聲說，『不然就叫他腦袋搬家，連你也一樣。』

「鐵齒布很快地退了回去。『噢，那樣的話……』

remove [rɪˋmuv] 動 脫掉

chop [tʃɑp] 動 砍《off》

dig [dɪg] 動 挖

desperately [ˋdɛspərɪtlɪ] 副 絕望地

stammer [ˋstæmɚ] 動 結結巴巴地說

'Some uncle, I thought bitterly.

'The guard drew out his mighty **sword** and swung it up above his head...But before he could bring it down, the door flew open and Princess Sarashina burst into the room.

'"What are you doing?" she cried. "Put that sword down at once. This is Tashi, the boy who **rescued** me from the demons and saved my life! Just as well I came back early, Tashi. What a way to **repay** your kindness." She **scolded** the Master of Revels and his guards out of the room.

「怎麼會有這種叔叔，我這麼想著，心裡很不是滋味。

「衛兵抽出他那把巨大的寶劍，高舉在頭上……但是還沒劈下來，莎拉喜娜公主就推開門闖了進來。

「『你們在搞什麼鬼？』她喊，『馬上把劍放下。這位就是大喜，就是他把我從惡魔手中救出來的！大喜，幸虧我回來得早。真是讓你好心沒好報。』她把寵臣和衛兵全都轟出房間。

sword [sɔrd] 名 劍
rescue [`rɛskju] 動 拯救
repay [rɪ`pe] 動 報答
scold [skold] 動 怒斥

'Well, I was never so glad to see anyone in my whole life. So when the Princess invited me to take tea with her, I followed her into a beautiful room all hung about with **silks** and tapestries, and we talked and laughed until nightfall.

'That evening I danced for the Emperor and the **Court**. I **twirled** high over people's heads and swooped and ducked and glided like a bird.

「我這輩子從來沒有這麼高興能見到某人。所以當公主邀我一起喝茶時，我就跟著她到一個很漂亮的房間，裡面掛滿了絲綢和織錦。我們又說又笑的一直到夜幕低垂。

　　「那天晚上我跳舞給皇上和滿朝文武大臣看。我向鳥一樣地在眾人頭上旋轉、俯衝、閃避、滑翔。

silk [sɪlk] 名 絲綢
Court [kɔrt] 名 朝臣
twirl [twɝl] 動 旋轉

'"Miraculous!" they cried, throwing coins at me, which Uncle Tiki Pu hastily **gathered** up. The Emperor gave me a nice little bag of gold for my trouble, but Tiki Pu was at my side at once. He **whisked** the bag from my hand.

'"I'll keep this safe for you, Tashi my boy," he **beamed**, as he slipped it into his pocket.

'"Is there anything else I can do for you, Tashi?" the Emperor asked.

'"Not for me, your Highness, but there is something my uncle would dearly like."

'Tiki Pu **pricked** up his ears and gave me a toothy grin.

「『太奇妙了』！他們喊著，對著我丟錢幣，鐵齒布叔叔很快地把錢幣收起來。皇帝也賞我一小袋黃金，以彌補我先前的委屈。不料鐵齒布卻立刻出現在我旁邊，一把將我手上的袋子搶走。

「『大喜，我的乖孩子，讓我來幫你保管。』他笑咪咪地將金子放進自己的口袋。

「『大喜，』皇帝問，『還有沒有什麼事是我能幫你做的？』

「『啟稟陛下，我已經別無所求，不過我叔叔非常想要某種東西。』

「鐵齒布豎起耳朵，對我露齒笑著。

gather [ˋgæðɚ] 動 收集
whisk [wɪsk] 動 迅速拿走
beam [bim] 動 微笑
prick [prɪk] 動 豎起 《up》

'"And what is that, my boy?" the Emperor smiled.

'"My uncle has always had a great desire to travel." Out of the corner of my eye I saw that Tiki Pu looked very surprised. I **whispered** something in the Emperor's ear.'

'What? What?' cried Dad.

'I know, I know!' cried Uncle Joe.

'Well, the next day I returned home **alone** and went straight at once to see Luk Ahed, the fortune teller. "You were right about the shoes," I said, "but I've had enough adventures for the time being, and I'm so tired. Can you tell me how to take them off?"

「『孩子，是什麼呢？』皇帝微笑著問。

「『我叔叔一直很想去旅行。』我用眼角瞥了鐵齒布一眼，他看起來很驚訝。我在皇帝耳邊說了幾句悄悄話。」

「說了什麼？說了什麼？」老爸叫著。

「我知道，我知道！」喬大叔也叫。

「隔天我獨自回家，馬上去找盧半仙，也就是那個算命仙。『關於那雙鞋子的事你都說對了。』我說，『可是這一趟下來，我已經受夠這些冒險了，而且我也累壞了。你能告訴我該怎麼把鞋子脫掉嗎？』」

whisper [ˋwɪspɚ] 動 低聲說

alone [əˋlon] 副 獨自地

'"Nothing could be easier," said Luk Ahed. "All you have to do is twirl around three times, clap your hands and say, Off shoes!"

'I followed his **instruction** and oh, the relief to wiggle my toes in the cool dust. I carried the shoes home and carefully put them in the bottom of my **playbox**.

'"And Tiki Pu hasn't come back with you?" my mother asked when I told her about the grand dinner and the Emperor and Princess Sarashina.

'"No, he couldn't. A **ship** was leaving the next morning for **Africa** and the Emperor thought that it was too good an **opportunity** for Tiki Pu to miss, seeing he likes travel so much."

「『再簡單不過了，』盧半仙說。『你只要轉三圈，拍拍手，然後說：脫鞋！』

「我按照他的指示做。哦，腳趾頭又能在涼爽的土地上活動，真是讓我鬆了一口氣。我把鞋子帶回家，小心翼翼地放在玩具箱底。

「當我告訴老媽關於那場晚宴、皇帝、還有莎拉喜娜公主的事時，她問我說，『鐵齒布沒跟你一塊兒回來嗎？』

「『沒有，他不能回來。隔天早上有一艘船要開往非洲，皇上知道鐵齒布熱愛旅行，認為他絕不能錯過這個天大的好機會。』

instruction [ɪn`strʌkʃən] 名 指示
playbox [`ple͵bɑks] 名 玩具箱
ship [ʃɪp] 名 船
Africa [`æfrɪkə] 名 非洲
opportunity [͵ɑpɚ`tjunətɪ] 名 機會

'My mother gave me one of her searching looks. "What a clever Tashi," she said at last, and smiled.'

There was a little **silence** at the table. Then Dad snorted loudly. 'Some uncle, all right, that Tiki Pu. Of all the lily-livered, cowardly...You wouldn't say *he* was a precious relative, would you, Tashi?'

'About as precious as a **crocodile** hanging off your leg!' put in Uncle Joe.

'He may have met a few by now,' grinned Tashi. 'Crocodiles are quite common in Africa, aren't they?'

'So I believe,' said Joe. 'In fact once, when I was in a typical African forest,

「我媽媽用銳利的眼神看了我一眼，最後笑著說，『大喜好聰明。』」

　　整桌子的人沈默了一會兒。然後老爸用鼻子很大聲地哼了一聲。「鐵齒布，唉，怎麼會有這種叔叔。真膽小，真沒出息⋯⋯大喜，你該不會說他是你寶貴的親人吧，會嗎？」

　　「大概跟攀在你大腿的鱷魚一樣寶貴！」喬大叔迸出一句。

　　「現在他可能已經碰到好幾隻了。」大喜笑著說。「鱷魚在非洲很常見，不是嗎？」

　　「沒錯，」喬大叔說，「事實上，以前有一次在典型的非洲森林時，

silence [ˋsaɪləns] 名 沉默
crocodile [ˋkrɑkəˌdaɪl] 名 鱷魚

I saw a crocodile **grab** the muzzle of a zebra.
Pulled him into the river, easy as blinking.
Dreadful sight. A Nile crocodile, it was.
Notorious man-killers. Did I tell you about the
time...?'

And so Tashi stayed till dusk crept in all over
the table and Dad had to put the lights on and
Tashi's mother called him home for dinner.

'Come back tomorrow, young fellow!' **urged**
Uncle Joe. 'I'm cooking *crocodile!*'

我就看過一隻鱷魚咬住一隻斑馬的嘴巴，把他拖進河裡，簡單得就像眨眼睛。很可怕的一幕。牠是尼羅河鱷魚，惡名昭彰的殺手。我有沒有跟你提過……？」

　　大喜就這樣一直待到天色暗了下來，整個餐桌都是漆黑一片，老爸必須開燈，大喜的媽媽也打電話來叫他回家吃晚飯。

　　「小伙子，明天再來！」喬大叔熱情地對大喜說。「我要煮鱷魚！」

grab [græb] 動 抓住

notorious [noˋtorɪəs] 形 惡名昭彰的

urge [ɝdʒ] 動 熱心地要求

嗨！我是大喜，
我常碰到許多有趣的事情唷！
想知道我的冒險故事嗎？

來自遠方的大喜／大喜愚弄噴火龍／大喜智取巨人／大喜與強盜
大喜妙計嚇鬼／前進白虎嶺／大喜與精靈／大喜與被擄走的小孩
大喜巧鬥巫婆／大喜妙懲壞地主／大喜勇退惡魔／大喜與奇妙鐘
大喜與大臭蟲／大喜與魔笛／大喜與寶鞋／大喜與算命仙

共 16 本，每本均附 CD

波波 唸翻天系列

你知道可愛的小兔子也會 "碎碎唸" 嗎？

波波就是這樣。

他將要告訴我們什麼有趣的故事呢？

波波的復活節／波波的西部冒險記／波波上課記
我愛你，波波／波波的下雪天／波波郊遊去
波波打球記／聖誕快樂，波波／波波的萬聖夜

共 9 本，每本均附 CD

全新的大喜故事來囉！這回大喜又將碰上什麼問□ 讓我們趕快來瞧瞧！

Anna Fienberg & Barbara Fienberg／著　Kim Gamble／繪　王秋□

大喜與奇妙鐘

哎呀呀！
村裡的奇妙鐘被河盜偷走了，
聰明的大喜
能幫村民們取回奇妙鐘嗎？

大喜與大臭蟲

可惡的大巨人！
不但吃掉人家的烤豬，
還吃掉人家的兒子。
大喜有辦法將巨人趕走嗎？

盟雄／譯

最新
出版

大喜與魔笛

糟糕！走了一群蝗蟲，
卻來了個吹笛人，
把村裡的孩子們都帶走了。
快來瞧瞧大喜是怎麼救回他們的！

最新
出版

大喜與算命仙

大喜就要死翹翹了！？
這可不妙！
盧半仙提議的方法，
真的救得了大喜嗎？

風和日麗，天高氣爽，
可愛的小動物們又要出來搗蛋囉！
這回他們又做了什麼？！

烏龍森林

小猴子幫森林裡的動物們洗衣服，
最後卻弄得雞飛狗跳！！！？？？

鱷魚巴索

可愛的鱷魚寶寶巴索老是把他的保姆氣跑，
這個新保姆也會一樣嗎？

龍龍查理
　　快醒來

恐龍查理老是從年頭睡到年尾，
　這個卻被森林裡的動物們吵醒了……

國家圖書館出版品預行編目資料

大喜與寶鞋 / Anna Fienberg,Barbara Fienberg著;Kim
　　Gamble繪;王盟雄譯.－－初版一刷.－－臺北市;
　　三民，民91
　　　面;公分--(探索英文叢書.大喜說故事系列;15)
　　中英對照
　　ISBN 957-14-3623-2　（平裝）

　　1. 英國語言—讀本

805.18

© 大喜與寶鞋

著作人　Anna Fienberg　Barbara Fienberg
繪　圖　Kim Gamble
譯　者　王盟雄
發行人　劉振強
著作財　三民書局股份有限公司
產權人　臺北市復興北路三八六號
發行所　三民書局股份有限公司
　　　　地址／臺北市復興北路三八六號
　　　　電話／二五○○六六○○
　　　　郵撥／○○○九九九八——五號
印刷所　三民書局股份有限公司
門市部　復北店／臺北市復興北路三八六號
　　　　重南店／臺北市重慶南路一段六十一號
初版一刷　中華民國九十一年四月
編　號　S 85611
定　價　新臺幣壹佰柒拾元整
行政院新聞局登記證局版臺業字第○二○○號

有著作權，不准侵害

ISBN　957-14-3623-2　（平裝）

網路書店位址：http://www.sanmin.com.tw